Praise for Ian Rankin

'As always, Rankin proves himself the master . . . there cannot be a better crime novelist' *Daily Mail*

'Whatever he writes, it will be worth reading' *Guardian*

'Real life and fiction blur . . . You'll love every second of it' *Daily Mirror*

'Ian Rankin is widely, and rightly, regarded as the leading male crime writer in Britain' *TLS*

'Ian Rankin . . . has produced yet another class act' *Evening Standard*

Ian Rankin was born in Scotland and graduated from the University of Edinburgh in 1982. He started to write fiction while studying. His first Inspector Rebus novel, *Knots & Crosses*, was published in 1987. The Rebus books are now translated into over thirty languages and are bestsellers around the world.

Ian Rankin has received many awards, including the Crime Writers' Association's Diamond Dagger. In 2002 he was awarded an OBE. He lives in Edinburgh with his partner and two sons. Visit his website at www.ianrankin.net.

By Ian Rankin

The Inspector Rebus series
Knots & Crosses
Hide & Seek
Tooth & Nail
Strip Jack
The Black Book
Mortal Causes
Let It Bleed
Black & Blue
The Hanging Garden
Dead Souls
Set in Darkness
The Falls
Resurrection Men
A Question of Blood
Fleshmarket Close
The Naming of the Dead
Exit Music

Other novels
The Flood
Watchman
Westwind
Doors Open

Short stories
A Good Hanging and Other Stories
Beggars Banquet

Non-fiction
Rebus's Scotland

A Cool Head

Ian Rankin

An Orion paperback

First published in Great Britain in 2009
by Orion Books Ltd
Orion House, 5 Upper St Martin's Lane,
London WC2H 9EA

An Hachette UK company

5 7 9 10 8 6

Quick Reads™ used under licence

A CIP catalogue record for this book
is available from the British Library.

ISBN 978-0-7528-8449-3

Typeset at the Spartan Press Ltd,
Lymington, Hants

Printed and bound in Great Britain by
Clays Ltd, St Ives plc

The Orion Publishing Group's policy is to use papers that
are natural, renewable and recyclable products and
made from wood grown in sustainable forests. The logging
and manufacturing processes are expected to conform to
the environmental regulations of the country of origin.

To Richard Havers, who took me to the Beach Boys concert where I got the idea for this story. They were singing a song about always keeping a cool head and a warm heart. I started to wonder about the opposite – a hot head and a heart as cold as stone.

Chapter One

Gravy's Story

My dad used to say to me, 'Try to keep a cool head and a warm heart.' At least, I think it was my dad. I don't really remember him. I've got a shoebox with photos in it, and in those photos he's always showing his teeth. I've rubbed my thumb over his face so much, he's become blurry, and that seems to be what's happened to my memories, too. They're fuzzy at the edges, and sometimes even fuzzy in the middle. If I went back to see Dr Murray, he'd tell me to start taking the pills again. But I don't like the pills. They make my head hot. My dad wouldn't like that. If he's still alive, he'll be fifty or sixty. I'm thirty, or something like that. Sometimes I stick my hand under my shirt just to check that my heart is still warm.

Cool head. Warm heart.

I remembered those words when I saw Benjy staggering towards me. He was holding a hand to his chest. His T-shirt was white mostly, but

1

with a lot of red. The red looked sticky and dark. There was a bag in his other hand, the kind you get at the grocer's shop, made of blue plastic.

I didn't recognise Benjy at first. What I saw was a car. It came in through the graveyard gates. There wasn't supposed to be a burial today, so I was a bit surprised. Visitors usually park on the gravel outside the gates. There's a big sign, PARKING FOR VISITORS. That was where visitors were supposed to park. But this car drove through the open gates. I wondered if I would get in trouble for leaving them open. I wondered who was in the car. It was a black car, nice and shiny. Maybe it belonged to someone official. The driver wasn't a good driver. He nearly hit one of the gravestones. The car kept hopping forwards, kangaroo petrol, they call it. That meant the driver was a learner, but I couldn't see any L-plates.

The car stopped and the door opened. Nobody got out at first. But then I saw a leg. And then another leg. And then the driver managed to get out of the car. He made a groaning sound, and that's when he pressed his hand to his chest. He left the door open and started walking towards me. I was collecting leaves and twigs and bunches of dead

2

flowers. They would all go on my bonfire. I had a wheelbarrow and a rake, and I was wearing my thick gloves.

'Gravy!'

It was when he said my name that I knew I was supposed to know him. His face and hair were covered in sweat. He had a denim jacket and his jeans had splashes on them. He was wearing an old pair of trainers. I was surprised to recognise Benjy. Benjy always wears a black leather coat. He always wears cowboy boots, and tight black trousers, and a black T-shirt. Today was different, for some reason.

'Gravy!'

Everyone calls me Gravy. It's got nothing to do with food. I can't really cook. Just micro-wave meals and things from the chip shop. Toast, I can make toast – and beans and fried eggs. But not lasagne or that sort of thing . . .

'Gravy!!!'

No, that's not why I got the name. It's short for graveyard, because that's where I work. And before I even worked here, I would come for walks here. I would read the people's stories on all the headstones. When they were born, where they lived and what their jobs were. I like all that stuff. And the bits of poems and prayers, and sometimes a carving or a photo.

3

Those photos always get damp, though, even when they're in plastic. They rot or they fade, like thoughts and memories – and people in the ground.

'Where's your coat?' I asked Benjy. He was near me now, only ten feet away. Or maybe twelve feet. He'd stopped walking and was bent over at the waist, as though tired.

'Never mind that,' he said. Then he tried to spit, but it was all gloopy and just hung there until he wiped it away with the bag hand – the hand carrying the bag. There was something heavy in the bag. Small but heavy. That's a good way of telling you about Benjy, too. He's small but heavy. He used to say he was a boxer. His punches would just miss my chin when he showed me. He wasn't really a boxer, but he knew about boxing. He went to matches and he watched videos of fights.

When he stopped bending over, he looked around, as if making sure there was no one else in the graveyard.

'Got something you want me to hide?' I asked. I'd hidden things for him before. Sometimes, weeks or months later, he asked for them back. Other times he didn't. That was how I met him the first time. He was hiding a bag behind a gravestone.

'Yeah,' Benjy said now. 'Me, for a start.' I didn't say anything. He made another of those groaning noises and tipped his head back. Then he said a swear word, and that made me a bit embarrassed. I looked away, leaning with one hand on my rake. The man who worked with me, my boss, had gone home ages ago, like most days. He told me what to do, and then went and sat in his hut with a newspaper or book, his radio, a flask of tea and some food. He usually threw away the sandwiches his wife made him and went to a baker's instead. He never gave the sandwiches to me, and never brought back anything for me from the shops. I waited until he went home, then I picked the sandwiches up off the compost heap. I always checked them to make sure there were no bugs or bits of leaf.

So, anyway, it was just me and Benjy in the graveyard. The sun had left the sky, so maybe it was time for me to go home too. I can't tell the time, so I have to guess these things. I do have a home, though. It's a room in a house. There are other people in the house. And if I lose track of time, one of them comes and fetches me, if they remember . . .

'Gravy? You paying attention?'

'Yes.'

'You need to pay attention.'

'Yes, Benjy.'

'I need to hide somewhere. How about your boss's hut?'

'Did he say it was all right?'

'Sure he did. I just spoke to him.'

'That's fine, then.'

'Is it locked?'

'He always locks it.'

'But you've got a key?'

I shook my head. I used to have a key, but then my boss found me sleeping in the hut one morning. I'd been there all night. It was so peaceful and quiet. Benjy was making a hissing sound. Then he started coughing, and the spit that came out of his mouth was pink, like he'd been eating sweets. He tried wiping it away again, but the bag was too heavy.

'I need to hide,' he repeated.

'Didn't he give you the key?'

'No.'

'That's a shame.' I thought for a moment. 'How about hiding behind the hedge?' I pointed to it. That's where the bonfires happen. It's where the compost is kept. And the digger. Not a big digger, but big enough for a hole six feet deep.

Benjy didn't seem to be listening. He fell to

his knees and I thought maybe he was going to pray. 'Tired,' was all he said.

'Yes,' I told him. 'You must be.'

He managed to look up at me. 'Nothing gets past you, Gravy.' Then he shoved the bag forward. It was sitting on the ground in front of him. 'Hide this for me.'

'Sure. Will you be wanting it back?'

'Not a chance.' His head slumped forward again. I could see his chest and shoulders rise and fall. He really was tired, so I left him there and tiptoed to a different part of the graveyard, and did some more raking.

It was almost dark by the time I got back to him. My wheelbarrow was empty. I'd left it with the rake next to the digger. I kept my gloves with me. They would go home with me. They were good gloves.

'Benjy? I've got to lock the gates now,' I said. 'Boss doesn't like them left open. People come in at night. They leave things lying around. Sometimes they paint things on the headstones or try to start fires. There's a big chain for the gates. Do you want me to move your car? Benjy?'

His shoulders weren't moving. He still looked like he was praying. My mum used to pray. She would be on her knees at the side of her bed, hands pressed together. I did the same thing, and sometimes I still do. But I always whisper the prayer so the other people in the house don't hear me.

'Benjy?'

I placed my hand on his shoulder and watched as he fell forwards until he was face down on the pathway. I knew what that meant. And when I turned him over, his eyes were closed, his mouth wide open. I pulled up his shirt and saw the hole in his chest. Blood had stopped coming out of it. His skin was cold to the touch.

'Bad,' I said. It was the first word that came into my head. 'Bad, bad, bad, bad.' Five times for luck. There was a dog barking somewhere. Dogs like the graveyard. So do cats and foxes and rabbits. Birds, too, in the daylight. I'd never seen or heard an owl. Or a bat or a rat or a mouse. One old lady from the estate told me there were badgers nearby, but she couldn't tell me where. She said she could smell them sometimes. I always wish I'd asked her what they smelled like, then I'd know.

'Bad badger, badger bad,' I said, liking the sound of it. Four more times for luck, then I looked inside the blue bag. It was a gun. It looked like a real gun. There was blood on the inside of the bag. The gun smelled of oil or grease. I'd hidden a knife for Benjy in the past, but never a gun. First time for everything, I thought to myself.

Then I noticed the car. There was a light on inside it, and that gave me a shock. But the door was open, and that had to be the reason. When you opened your door, a little light came on. I walked over to the car and looked inside. More sticky blood on the seat and the steering wheel, and a balaclava on the floor. The key was in the ignition. The car smelled of leather, and there was a little green tree hanging below the mirror. Benjy had forgotten his other bag. It was the kind people carried when they were going to play football or visit the pool. It was red and shiny and, when I opened it, it was full of bits of paper. I lifted out one of the bundles and held it up to the little light in the car's ceiling.

It was money.

The notes all had 20 on them. That meant each one was worth twenty pounds. I put the bundle back in the bag and looked through the windscreen. Benjy was still there. So was the blue bag with the gun inside. He wanted me to hide the gun. But what about the car? What about the red bag?

And what about Benjy?

Chapter Two

George Renshaw's Scrapyard

'I'm not happy,' Gorgeous George said.

This was true. But then he wasn't gorgeous either. As Don Empson stared at his employer, he wondered how George had ended up with the nickname. Maybe it was ironic, a sort of joke. Like calling a glum bloke in the pub 'Smiler'. Gorgeous George was as wide as he was tall, and he wasn't exactly short. He always wore his shirtsleeves rolled up. His arms were hairy, with a lot of tattoos. The tattoos were from his days in the Royal Navy. There were thistles and pipers and naked women. George was completely bald. His scalp gleamed. There were nicks and scars on it, and more scars on his face and neck. He wore a large gold ring on each and every finger, right hand and left, plus a heavy gold ID bracelet on one wrist and a gold Rolex watch on the other. When he laughed, which didn't happen very often, you could see a couple of gold teeth towards the back of his mouth. His eyes were small, almost childlike, and he had no eyebrows. His nose was red and pulpy, like an overripe strawberry. He sat behind his desk and drummed its surface with his jewelled fingers.

'Not happy at all,' he said.

'You're not the only one,' Don told him. 'How do you think I feel? Nice easy job you said. A simple delivery. I mean, someone sticks a gun in my face. I'm not happy either.'

Okay, so it had been his stomach rather than his face, but Don reckoned face would sound better.

'Time was,' George muttered, 'you'd have taken that gun away from him and slapped him about a bit.'

'Time was,' Don agreed. It was true, he was getting old. He'd worked for George's dad for the best part of thirty years. When Albert had died and George had taken over the business, Don had reckoned he'd be put out to pasture. But George had wanted him around, 'a link to the old days'. Don hadn't been keen, not that he'd said anything.

And now this.

'You sure you didn't recognise him?' George asked again.

'He was wearing a mask.'

'And he was on his own?'

'As far as I could see.'

'And there were three of you? Three against one?'

'Looked to me like he was the only one holding a shooter.' Don paused. 'Are you sure we should be discussing this here?'

He meant bugs. George was worried the cops had planted bugs in his office. George scowled at Don's question, but then thought about it and nodded. 'Let's take a walk,' he said, rising to his feet.

The office was a Portakabin and the Portakabin stood in the middle of a scrapyard. Don was wary. He knew what those words could mean, *let's take a walk*. Didn't always end well for people, the walks they took in this scrapyard, walks they took with Gorgeous George.

Don's shoulders and arms were tensed as they stepped outdoors. The crane, the one with the big magnet swinging from its arm, had finished work for the day. The compactor sat in silence. In the past, it had crushed its fair share of cars. Sometimes those cars had contained evidence . . . and sometimes body parts.

'I've told you,' Don said to his boss, 'I'm getting too old for this. World's changing too fast. It's younger guys like Sam and Eddie you should be relying on.'

'But it comes down to trust in the end, Don,' George replied, 'and I wouldn't trust either of them the way I trust you. My dad always told me, "Don's the guy. Any problems, Don'll sort things out." '

'All in the past, George.'

George had slung an arm around Don's shoulders. They were walking past the German Shepherds. The two huge dogs stared at them, tongues lolling from their mouths. But they didn't bark. They knew better than to bark at George. If Don was on his own, they'd be straining at the leash, keen to sink their teeth into a leg or an arm. But right now, George was protecting him.

The two men were heading into the heart of the scrapyard. Cars and other vehicles were piled on top of each other. Many had been hauled here from the scenes of accidents. People would have died in those accidents. People would have lost limbs and loved ones.

'So tell me again,' George said. 'Tell me how it all happened.'

Don thought for a moment and took a deep breath. 'Well,' he said, 'I drove into the garage, like you told me. Hanley wasn't there yet, so it was just me and Raymond. Raymond was working on a Bentley, polishing the dashboard, really doing a thorough job . . .'

'He's a car valet. That's what he does.'

'Not any more.'

George managed a sympathetic look. 'Not any more,' he agreed.

'So anyway, I was talking to him, just the usual stuff . . . and then Hanley arrives. He drives on to the forecourt but leaves his car there, keeps the engine running. He wasn't planning on sticking around. The bag was in the front seat of my car. Should only have taken us two minutes . . .'

'So when did the bandit arrive?'

'He came out of nowhere. Balaclava pulled down over his face. Just a couple of holes for the eyes and one for the mouth. He was carrying a pistol. Funny thing is . . .'

'What?'

'Well, I had this wild thought when I saw him. I wondered if you'd sent him.'

'Me?'

'That way you'd get your money back, and Hanley couldn't complain. He'd still have to keep his side of the deal.'

George was shaking his head. But he was

thinking too. Don reckoned he knew what he was thinking, *Wish I'd thought of that* . . .

'And you just handed the cash over to him?' George asked.

'I'm not a martyr, George. The gun was real.'

'So how did the shooting start?'

'There were the three of us, me, Hanley and the mask. Nobody was paying attention to Raymond. He must have had the gun tucked away somewhere. He shot twice. It was deafening.'

'And he got the guy?'

'First bullet went wide, second one hit him in the chest.' Don paused for a moment. It was painful for him, remembering this. He made a show of clearing his throat. 'But by then he'd fired back at Raymond. Went straight into his skull and he dropped. The money was still in my car, so the mask got into the driver's seat and backed out of the garage. Headed across the forecourt and was gone.'

'Before you could pick up Raymond's gun?'

Don just shrugged.

'What did Hanley do? Besides wetting himself, I mean.'

'He ran back to his car and hightailed it.'

'Same direction the bandit took?'

Don shook his head. 'You reckon Hanley . . . ? But he was going to get the money anyway.'

George thought about this and nodded. He folded his arms. 'This isn't good, Don. How did you get out of there?'

'Well, the Bentley had its keys in.'

'Where is it now?'

'Parked up behind the Portakabin. Reckon it needs to go in the compactor?'

'Of course it does!'

'Shame. Raymond did a beautiful job of cleaning it.'

'Well, Raymond was a pro, wasn't he?' George gave Don a look, as if to say, *And I thought you were too.*

'I've never shot anyone in my life, George. In the old days, fists were enough, maybe a bottle or a knife now and again.'

'These aren't the old days.' George thought for another moment. 'I need to talk to Hanley, make sure he's okay. Meantime, *you* need to find your car. And there's still that other little matter to be taken care of.'

Don nodded. 'What about our bandit friend?'

'He's wounded, maybe badly wounded. He's got to have ended up in hospital.' George jabbed a finger at Don. 'So start making some calls.'

'Then we pay him a visit?'

George just nodded. 'Was Raymond married? Is there someone we should send flowers to?'

'I don't know.'

'Find out, will you?'

'Before or after the other matter?'

George glowered at him. 'What do you think? No, never mind what *you* think. Whoever was wearing that mask, they knew the cash was being handed over. That means it's someone we know, or someone Hanley knows. It means someone somewhere has blabbed or else got greedy. It means they're *close*, Don. And if they're close, we're going to have no trouble finding them.'

Don nodded his agreement. Thing is, George, he thought to himself, *you don't know* how *close*.

'When do we tell Stewart?' he asked.

'When I'm ready,' George snarled, marching back towards his dogs and the Portakabin.

Don waited for another minute, then headed in the same direction. The German Shepherds snarled and spat, baring their teeth. They were up on their back legs, front legs off the ground and pawing at the air, willing their studded collars to break. Don ignored them and headed for the Bentley. He didn't know whose car it was. There was some dust on the windows and a bit of mud on the tyres. Plus some of Raymond's blood and brain matter on the right-side wing. A wipe would get rid of it. Or a hose, if you wanted to be really careful. But the inside of the car was clean, immaculate in fact. He considered his options. But if he kept it, it would be noted as missing, and the cops would assume Raymond's killer had taken it. No, Gorgeous George was right, it had to be turned into scrap. Shame, though.

But Don had plenty of other problems. He knew he should be angry, but all he really felt was sorrow. There was no way out, that was the truth of it.

No happy ending.

Chapter Three
Gravy's Story (2)

It took me a while to find her house. I don't know that part of the city. Benjy's car had one of those little map-readers, but I didn't know how to work it. I can drive a car, though, not much different from dodgems. Benjy's was an automatic. Those are the cars I can drive. So I drove to her address. The piece of paper was in the glove box. Why is it called that, a glove box? I tried it with my own gloves, but they wouldn't fit without squashing them, and I didn't want to do that. But I found the piece of paper and it had her name on it, plus her address. She was called Celine Watts. I stopped the car beside some kids on bikes and showed them her address. They shook their heads. Then I tried at a bus stop and a man pointed up the road. So then I got lost a few times but a woman on her way home from the shops told me exactly what to do. Right, and right again. I write with my right hand, that's a good way to remember left from right.

Ten Merchant Crescent was a council house on a council estate. But there wasn't too much graffiti and no supermarket trolleys or burned-out cars. It was quite nice, really. I parked the car by the kerb and had to work out how to use the hand brake. Then I walked up her path and pushed the bell. I didn't hear any noise from inside, so I tried again. Then I knocked instead, and a voice called out from behind the door.

'Who's there?' It was a woman's voice.

'I'm Gravy,' I called back. 'I've come about Benjy.' See, the thing was, I needed to tell someone. I needed someone to know what I knew.

'Who?'

'Benjy. Your friend Benjy.'

'I don't have a friend called Benjy.'

I looked at the piece of paper. 'It says Celine Watts.'

'It's pronounced Se-leen,' she called out. Then the door opened an inch and I could see a bit of her face and one of her eyes. 'Who are you?'

'I'm Gravy. A pal of Benjy's. Look.' I held the paper up so she could read it. 'It was in his car, and now he's . . . he's had a bit of an accident.'

21

She stared hard at the piece of paper, and then her eyes met mine. 'Who sent you?' she asked. She sounded scared.

'Nobody sent me.'

'Are you going to kill me?'

'No.' I think I sounded properly shocked.

'You don't look like you are.'

'I'm not.'

'But I don't know anyone called Benjy.'

'He had your name in his car.' I pushed the piece of paper closer to her.

'So I see.' The door had opened another couple of inches. I could see more of her now. Her hair was brown and short. Her face was round and shiny. Her eyes were green. 'So this friend of yours called Benjy, he had my name and address in his car?'

I nodded, and she looked over my shoulder.

'Is that his car or yours?' she asked.

'His, I suppose.'

'You suppose?'

'Well, it's not his usual car. His usual car is green, a bit like your eyes.'

She almost smiled. 'And what's happened to Benjy?' The door was all the way open now.

'He's not very well.'

'Who is he? What's his last name?'

'I don't know his last name.'

'Do you work with him?'

'No.' I paused while I had a think. 'I don't know where he works. But he must have a job because he always has money.' Then I corrected myself. 'Always *had* money, I mean.'

Her eyes narrowed. 'Are you saying he's dead?'

I sniffed and rubbed my nose. 'I suppose so,' I said. Celine Watts lifted the piece of paper from my fingers.

'And you found this in his car?'

'Yes.'

'But it's not the car he usually drives?' She was looking over my shoulder again. 'How did he die?'

'I don't know.' I think she could see that I was lying. 'Do you mind if I take a look?'

'A look at what?'

'A look at the car.' She squeezed past me, leaving her door wide open. I wanted to tell her that all the heat would escape, it was the sort of thing my mum would say. But instead, I followed her. She opened the passenger door. 'Area like this, you should have locked it,' she said. She was opening the glove box.

'My gloves wouldn't fit,' I explained, but she wasn't listening. She took out a book and started turning its pages. It had drawings of all the parts of the car. But at the back there was another piece of paper, folded in four. She opened it up.

'It's a bill,' she said, 'for fixing the car.' Then she stopped speaking. There was a gurgling sound in her throat. Her mouth stayed open.

'Gravy,' she said, 'do you know a man called Donald Empson?'

I shook my head. 'Is this his car?'

'I think so,' she said. 'It's his name on the bill.'

'And you know him?'

She placed a hand to her chest, as if to check her heartbeat. Warm heart, cool head. 'I know who he is,' she said quietly. 'Are you sure you don't know how your friend Benjy died?'

'I think someone killed him.' Tears were coming into my eyes. I wiped them away.

'He was a friend of yours?'

'Yes.' I repeated it four more times for luck. She seemed to be thinking about things, staring into the distance. Then she turned her attention to the open door of her house.

'Police told me I'd be safe,' she said. She shook her head slowly. We stood together in silence for a minute, and then she asked me what was in the bag. It was on the floor in front of the passenger seat.

'It's not mine,' I said.

She was already unzipping it. When she looked inside, she saw my gloves first, but then she saw what was beneath them and she placed the hand to her chest again.

'It's Benjy's money,' I explained. 'I don't know what to do with it. I was hoping you'd be a friend of his . . .'

She looked at me and then smiled. It was a big, beaming smile, and it was followed by a laugh.

'I *am* a friend of Benjy's,' she said, taking my arm and squeezing it. 'This was supposed to be my surprise.' She nodded towards the bag. 'And now you've delivered it. Thank you, Gravy!'

I was a bit confused. 'The bag's for you?'

'It's money for my holiday.'

I thought about it, but it still wasn't clear. It seemed all fuzzy in the middle.

'I need to be going,' she was saying. 'Quite soon, Gravy.' She was looking at the open door again. 'I just need to pack a few . . . no, maybe not. I can buy whatever I need. No passport, though.' She bit her bottom lip. 'Passport's at my flat.'

'Is this not your house?'

'My cousin's. Police called it a "safe house", fat lot they know. I've only been here two days, and Don Empson's got the address.' She looked around us, suddenly fearful. 'Need to get out of here, Gravy,' she decided. 'Somewhere safe. Can you drive?' She realised what she'd said and laughed a short laugh. 'What am I saying? You drove here, didn't you?'

'I did,' I said.

'So maybe you can give me a lift?'

'The bus stop?' I guessed, but she shook her head.

'Edinburgh.'

'That's miles. We could run out of petrol.'

'We've got money,' she said, grabbing my arm again. 'Plenty of money, remember? My holiday money.'

And with that, she lifted out the bag, then got into the car, resting it on her lap.

'Are you going to leave the door open?' I asked, pointing towards the house. 'The heat will get out.'

'Let it,' she snapped. But she could see I wasn't happy. 'The rooms need airing,' she explained. 'Place gets stuffy otherwise. Now come on.' She patted the driving seat. 'I want your best Jeremy Clarkson impression.'

'Who?'

She sighed and rolled her eyes. 'Just get in and drive, Gravy.'

'I don't know Edinburgh. I've never been there.'

'We'll take the motorway. Don't worry, you won't get lost.' Her face went sad again. 'Unless you don't want to help a friend of Benjy's. If you don't want to help me, just say so.'

But I did want to help her. I wanted to see her smile again. It was a good smile. A smile like my mum's.

'Okay,' I said.

Chapter Four

Don Empson is Hunting

Jim Gardner was Benjy's best friend. When Don Empson left him, he was bleeding and weeping. Don didn't think Jim knew anything about anything. But he'd asked him questions all the same. Who else did Benjy know? Who might he go to for help? And Jim had done a lot of talking. Don felt bad about it, felt he'd worked out a lot of his own anger on Gardner. That was hardly professional.

Don had been busy since leaving the scrapyard. He'd borrowed one of the cars. It made noises that warned him it was dying.

'You and me both,' he'd told it. In his case this was certainly true. Six months, the hospital had told him. Maybe a year with treatment, but his quality of life would suffer. He'd spend half his time on a trolley in the hospital corridor.

'No thanks,' he'd said. 'Just give me painkillers, lots of painkillers.'

There were some in his pocket right now, but

the only things that hurt were his knuckles. Jim Gardner had told him there was this graveyard, out by the old blocks of flats. Some bloke there, Benjy said he was useful. He would hide things for him.

All sorts of things.

Gardner didn't know the man's name, but that didn't matter. On his way to the grave-yard, Don called his friend in the police. For the price of a few drinks, his friend would put out a call to all patrol cars. They would keep their eyes open for Don's car, the one Benjy had taken. For another few drinks, this same friend would ask all the hospitals in the area if anyone had been brought in wounded.

'Wounded?' the cop had asked.

'Don't worry,' Don had told him. 'It's not anyone who didn't deserve it.' He didn't want to spook the cop.

But when Don called from the car, there was no news. He reached the graveyard in twenty minutes. It was even closer to Raymond's gar-age, maybe twelve or fifteen minutes. No dis-tance at all. The gates were closed. He got out and checked them. They were held shut by a chain. Don peered through the bars but couldn't see any signs of life.

'Just signs of death,' he said to himself. He

had already planned his own funeral, a cremation with music by Johnny Cash.

If he lived that long. He thought of the compactor and had to shake the image away. He looked around him. There were some kids further up the hill, gathered around a couple of bikes by a lamp post. Don drove towards them and stopped the car. He got out again. Twenty pounds, a fiver for each kid, and he had some more information. The guy who worked in the graveyard was called Gravy. He was 'not all there'. Don listened, and then described his own car. There were nods. Then he described Benjy. More nods.

'Did you see the car leave?' The boys couldn't really remember, until another twenty had changed hands.

'Never seen anything as funny in my life,' one of them said. The others were smiling at the memory.

'Gravy, trying to drive!' He burst out laughing, and his friends joined in.

'Any idea where he was going?'

They shook their heads.

'And no sign of the other guy?'

They shook their heads again.

Don just nodded slowly and wondered if another twenty might help. Probably not. So he saved his money and got back into the dying car. Could the money be in the graveyard? Could Benjy be in the graveyard? Don turned the car around. The boys were walking away. They gave him a wave. He waved back and pressed his foot a little harder on the pedal. The car hit the gates and snapped the chain. The gates flew open. Don kept driving, aware that, somewhere behind him, the boys were cheering and clapping. He did a circuit of the graveyard, but couldn't see anything unusual. He stopped the car and got out. There was a hut, but it was padlocked shut. It had a window with wire mesh covering it. He looked inside, but there was no sign of life. Behind a hedge, he found a digger and a wheelbarrow, but nothing else. He stood there in the darkness, scratching his head.

And that was what he was doing when the police car arrived.

It took him an hour to talk his way out of it. They took him to the police station. The desk sergeant knew who he was, and didn't believe his story. Some kids, joyriders, smashing their way through the gates and then running off . . . Don Empson, concerned citizen, completely innocent, checking the scene.

'I wanted to make sure they hadn't damaged anything.'

'So the car's not yours, sir?'

'Never seen it in my life.'

When they let him go, he breathed the cold night air and took his phone out of his pocket. Nothing else for it. He would have to bring in Sam and Eddie. They always travelled together. They'd been best pals since primary school, nutters, the pair of them. But that wasn't really the problem. Problem was, he couldn't let them know what *he* knew. He couldn't let them know Benjy was the shooter.

Because Benjy was family. He was *Don's* family, his nephew. And if Don didn't get to him first, the lad was as good as dead. Always supposing he wasn't dead already. Don felt a stabbing pain in his stomach. He rubbed at it, for all the good that would do. *Benjy, you bloody idiot.* No happy ending.

He thought back to the garage, how it had taken him a couple of seconds to recognise Benjy's build and voice. He'd been on the point of saying something when the first shot had rung out. And afterwards, just for a moment, Benjy's wide, scared eyes had met his. Then he'd screwed his eyes shut. Chest wound. Should Don have stopped him driving off? Should he have called out, *Let me get you to a doctor*? Probably. The question now was, had Benjy known it would be his uncle in charge of the cash? If so, he'd gambled either that he wouldn't be recognised, or that Don wouldn't grass him up.

Big gamble.

It came down to that moment of eye contact. There had been no surprise there, so Benjy *had* expected Don, and, furthermore, had expected to be clocked by him . . .

Happy to land his uncle in the mire.

'Cuts both ways, lad,' Don said to the night air, rubbing his stomach again.

Chapter Five

Stewart Renshaw's Casino

Stewart Renshaw was in one of his casinos when he got a call from his brother.

'George,' he said into the phone. 'Did everything go as planned?'

The silence on the other end of the line was enough of an answer. Stewart's face tightened and he decided the gaming floor was too public. There were only a few punters in, but it was still early, not quite midnight. He pushed open a door marked PRIVATE and entered a hallway used by the staff. There was nobody around.

'Talk to me, George,' he said.

'There was a bit of trouble,' Gorgeous George finally owned up. 'Someone came in with a gun, shot Raymond and took the cash.'

'Is Raymond all right?'

'Funeral job.'

Stewart leaned against the door and closed his eyes. 'What about Hanley?'

'Nobody else got hurt . . . except the shooter.'

'Is he dead, too?'

'Raymond shot him in the chest. He won't get far.'

'But he's got my money?'

'Yes.'

'And you told me it was a piece of cake!' Stewart hissed. 'Don't tell me you sent Sam and Eddie?'

'Don Empson.'

'He's well past his sell-by date.'

'Dad always liked him.'

'Dad's in the past, George. All of that's in the past.' Stewart ran a hand through his hair, trying to think. He was tall and thin and didn't look at all like George. This had led him to wonder, had their mum had an affair? George looked like their dad, but not Stewart. Bit late to do anything about it, but all the same . . . it might explain a few things.

'So what are you going to do?' he asked.

'Check the hospitals. Shooter took Don's car, so we're looking for that, too. But can you talk to Hanley, see how he's doing?'

'I'll talk to him. But don't forget, it's *my* money, George. Someone's got to pay.'

'Okay, Stewart. Is the club busy tonight?'

'Dead.'

'It'll get better.'

Stewart wanted to slap his brother, wanted to punch him in his soft, fat face. But he wouldn't. He was a proper businessman these days. He had to keep his distance from everything in his past.

He had to stay clean.

He ended the call and gave the nearest wall a couple of butts with his head. What did he do now, phone Hanley or visit him in person? How could he visit him when his driver hadn't turned up for work yet? And besides, the whole point of using George's guys for the handover was so he himself could steer clear of Hanley.

It was cleaner that way.

'If a job needs doing,' he muttered to himself. He went to the main office and asked if anyone had seen Benjy Flowers. There were shrugs and shakes of the head.

'As useless as his bloody Uncle Don.' Then, to the room: 'Soon as he gets here, send him along.' Leaving the room, Stewart reached into his pocket for his phone.

The home of Councillor Andrew Hanley

Andrew Hanley was back home, seated in a chair in his darkened study with a glass of whisky in one hand. He still had the shakes. His wife was downstairs. When he'd come home, she'd called to him from the kitchen. He'd called back, but made his way up the stairs and into his study, closing the door after him. When the door was closed, she wouldn't come in. It meant he was working. The only light came from the lamp post directly outside the window. He could see his desk, covered with paperwork. His degree was framed on the wall. So were photos of him meeting important people, people from sports and TV and business. As a city dignitary, he got to meet lots of people.

But he wished now that he'd never met Stewart Renshaw.

It had all been very friendly at first, very sociable. He accepted an invite to dinner at one of Stewart's casinos. He accepted some free gaming chips. Then there was another visit, and more chips. The place seemed well run. It wasn't full of gangsters or lowlifes. It was respectable. Okay, so Stewart was Albert Renshaw's son, and Albert's nickname had been

'The Godfather'. But Stewart had washed his hands clean of all that. He never saw his kid brother George; spoke to him twice a year. Stewart was above board, or seemed so at first.

There had been a day at the races, again as Stewart's guest. 'Bring the wife,' he'd been told. But he'd lied and said she was busy. He wanted an adventure all of his own. He met good-looking women. He met friendly and powerful men. He had a good time. Once, he was offered drugs, a snort of cocaine in the toilets, but he refused. Champagne was quite enough for him.

Back then, it had all seemed enough.

His phone started to vibrate. He lifted it from his pocket and looked at the screen. It was Stewart. Hanley decided not to answer. What was he going to say to the man? It had crossed his mind that the whole thing was a set-up, some sort of play being acted out, so as to cheat him out of the money. But the guns and the blood had seemed real. The fear and the anger had seemed real. Not just special effects, but blood and smoke and the flash from the two guns. And such loud bangs. Three of them. He'd run to his car, hitting another vehicle as he reversed at speed. He had fled the scene of a crime, the scene of a murder. Him: Councillor

Andrew Hanley. Head of Planning. And now this . . .

No, he would not answer his phone. He would not speak to Stewart Renshaw. He would drink his whisky and stare at the wall. Then his wife called to him from the bottom of the stairs.

'Andrew?'

He didn't answer.

'Andrew?'

But then that might make her suspicious.

'Andrew?'

'What is it?'

'Your shoes.' Yes, his shoes, he had left them just inside the front door. It was one of Lorna's rules, no shoes in the house.

'What about them?'

'Did you step in something? Some red stuff?'

Red stuff! Yes, red stuff! Blood, blood, blood!

'It's paint,' he called out to her. 'That's all, just some paint.'

'Shall I try cleaning it off?'

'No, I'll do it. I'll do it later.'

There was silence from downstairs. Then: 'Do you want any supper?'

'I just want to be left alone! Is that too much to ask?'

This time, the silence had no end. Hanley tried to lift the remains of the whisky to his mouth, but his hand was shaking too much.

Chapter Six

Don Empson is Still Hunting

Sam was driving. Eddie was in the seat next to him. Don sat in the back, not saying much. He had explained that he wanted to visit Raymond's garage. Well, not *visit* it exactly, just cruise past it. As they turned into the narrow back street, Eddie cleared his throat and said a single word.

'Cops.'

Three patrol cars had formed a roadblock. Tape was being strung between lamp posts. A couple of white vans were parked, a team emerging from them. They wore overalls and carried face masks. The forensics crew. A uniformed cop was making signals with his hand. Sam nodded and did a U-turn.

'What do you want to do?' he asked.

'Let's check some of the other streets,' Don told him.

'What happened at Raymond's?' Eddie asked.

'Somebody shot him,' Don explained. Eddie

whistled but didn't say anything. Sam met Don's eyes in the rear-view mirror, but didn't say anything either. They drove in silence, cruising up one street and down another. Workshops and offices, then some tenements with shops below. There was no one about, but Don knew that soon the police would be knocking on doors, armed with their questions. Shots had been heard. Someone had rung 999. He remembered that he had another piece of business. The middle of the night might be a good time for it. But first, he had to keep his eyes open. He was looking for a car, a green sports car. Benjy's car. And eventually he saw it. It was parked two streets away from the garage. There was a half-filled skip next to it. He managed not to look too interested. He didn't want Sam and Eddie knowing more than they needed to know.

Benjy's plan: grab the money and run back to the car.

Benjy's plan hadn't worked out.

Don knew that the police would spot the car eventually. Or someone would draw it to their attention. After which they could run a quick check and come up with the name Benjamin Flowers. They would ask Benjy's mother, Don's sister, what Benjy did for a living, and she would tell them. *He works for Stewart Renshaw.* Stewart, brother of George. And then George would know, and he would blame it all on Don. Giving Benjy a job had been a favour to Don. Someone would have to pay for that.

Don would have to pay.

He had gone through a whole range of emotions. Anger at Benjy, then sadness, and finally acceptance. Stuff happened, you just had to deal with it as best you could. But right now, he didn't know what would count as best.

As Sam took a right turn, Don leaned forward and told him there was a new destination, Merchant Crescent.

'I'm going to have a word with someone,' he added. 'Guess what her name is.'

Sam was the first to twig. 'Celine Watts?'

'Got it in one.'

'Are we going to whack her?' Eddie asked.

'Would that be wise?' Don snapped back. 'And besides, *you* are going nowhere near her. Like I said, I'm going to have a quiet word, that's all. See if I can persuade her to change her story.'

Sam was looking at him in the mirror again. 'Thanks, Mr Empson,' he said.

'The one you should be thanking is Gorgeous George.'

Sam nodded slowly. He knew the score. The pair of them had been spotted in a car park next to woodland on the edge of the city. There had been another man in the car with them and he'd been crying, according to the witness. The witness was Celine Watts. The crying man was a small-time pusher who'd been warned before. His body had been found in the woods, in too shallow a grave.

Leaving Gorgeous George three options. Option one, hang Sam and Eddie out to dry. Option two, get them off the hook. Option three, bump them off.

So far, it had been option two.

The streets were quiet. It only took them half an hour. Eddie stopped the car next to the kerb and Don started to get out.

'Do you need us?' Eddie asked.

'Not on your life.' Don pulled on a pair of black leather gloves and walked up the path. When he got to the front door, he noticed that it was open a couple of inches. There were lights on inside. He pushed at the door and stepped into the narrow hallway. The first door led to the living room. Music was playing, and he could smell smoke. A woman was lying on the sofa, her feet bare. She was moving her toes in time to the music. There was an empty bottle of lemonade on the floor, next to a bottle of vodka. She was flicking ash from her cigarette into the palm of her hand.

She was not Celine Watts.

'You're not Celine,' he said.

She showed no surprise at his arrival. Her eyes were glassy. She blew some smoke towards him.

'Her cousin,' she explained. 'Sofa's supposed to be where she sleeps.' There was a sleeping bag rolled up under the woman's head. 'Only she's done a runner. Left the front door wide open and everything. Lucky nobody nicked my stereo.'

'Maybe she's with the police,' Don said.

'Are *you* not the police?' She watched him shake his head, then concentrated on her cigarette again. 'Neighbour saw her driving away in a flash car. A black, shiny car. Looked official.'

'What did the driver look like?'

The woman shrugged. Don's BMW, the one Benjy had taken, was black. And some people would call it flash. It was a 7 Series.

And this address was in the glove box.

Had Benjy come here to warn Celine Watts? Unlikely, the state he'd have been in. And anyway, the kids on the street had told him it was the guy called Gravy. Gravy, panicking at the sight of Benjy covered in blood. Gravy, finding the address and assuming it to be a safe house of sorts. Finding Celine Watts instead.

Gravy, with Don's car. With Celine Watts. With Stewart's money.

'Where would she go?' he asked the cousin. Her eyelids were drooping.

'Far away from here, if she's got any sense.'

Don knew he would have to call his pal at the cop shop again and ask him to widen the search. 'Did she take all her stuff?' he asked the cousin. She shook her head.

'Didn't take *anything*. Her bag, purse, phone, toothbrush, they're all still here. This is even her vodka I'm drinking.' As she reached down for her glass, the little collection of cigarette ash fell from her hand.

'Cheers,' she said. Then she lost her balance, rolled off the sofa and landed on the floor, laughing. Don ignored her and opened the shoulder bag on the coffee table. Celine Watts' purse was inside, along with aspirin and paper hankies and a phone. Why hadn't she taken anything? Because she'd been scared. And besides, she had everything she needed in the car . . . a driver, and a small mountain of cash.

The cousin was still chuckling quietly to herself, eyes closed. He knew that if he beat her up, it would send a message to Celine Watts. The sort of message Gorgeous George would thank him for.

All the same, Don didn't have the heart for it. He pocketed Celine's purse and phone and walked back to the waiting car.

Chapter Seven
The Detective

Jane Harris had been a detective inspector for all of three weeks, and here she was standing in a garage with pools of blood at her feet.

Pools plural.

The cold, dead victim was called Raymond Masters. It was his garage. He cleaned cars for a living, or had done until about four hours ago. That was how long it had taken them to locate the source of the gunshots. A gun had been found in the dead man's hand, and it had been fired. It wasn't suicide, though. Two shots had been fired by Masters. One bullet had already been located, stuck in the wall to the left-hand side of the doors. One had done some damage to another human, if the bloodstains were to be believed. There were big dollops of the stuff. Masters had suffered a shot to the head. There should have been a spray of blood and brain matter, but cars had been parked here. Probably two of them, judging by the tyre marks.

Jane Harris had asked one of her team to look in Masters' office. He would have bookings. She wanted to know which car or cars he had been working on. Maybe someone had wanted them. Cars got stolen all the time, didn't they? But carjackers didn't normally resort to guns. And why had the garage owner carried a gun of his own?

Her colleague Bob Sanders had a different theory. Bob had been on the force for almost as long as Jane had been alive. She trusted him when he mentioned the name George Renshaw.

'Explain,' was all she said, folding her arms.

'Raymond might look clean these days, but in the past he was a bit of a lad. Ran with Albert Renshaw's crew. Albert was George's dad. Raymond's done time inside. Word is that he's still friends with Gorgeous George, and I can see why he'd be useful . . . George might sometimes have a car that needs cleaning.'

'I thought he got rid of them at his scrapyard.'

'Maybe.'

Bob left her to think about it. He knew she *would* think about it. The guy who'd been wounded . . . someone would know. A doctor or hospital. An all-night supermarket where he could buy compresses and bandages. Someone would know. Or he could be nearby, hiding, biding his time. Maybe in a garden or a flat. He could have burst his way in. Jane knew that the first few hours were crucial, knew that the trail started to go cold after that. She needed people to go knocking on doors. She needed at least a couple of sniffer dogs.

One member of the forensic team was taking a photo of a footprint. The footprint was bloody. It got fainter as it neared the garage doors. The wounded man? No, because he'd been twelve feet further away. But the pool of blood vanished too. There were no signs that it led outside. So, one man heading outside, one man taking a car. Had they been partners? Or was one a bystander?

'Might be a car theft after all,' another detective said, emerging from the office. 'Full valet this afternoon on a big Bentley. They cost a hundred grand plus. Owner's number's in the diary. I've just talked to him. He was picking the car up in the morning.'

'Put out a call,' Jane said. 'Let everyone know the registration. Box of chocolates for the first one who spots it.'

'And a hug and a kiss from yourself, Jane?' Bob joked.

'Unless you're the winner,' she told him. Another officer had appeared from the forecourt.

'Parked car, recently damaged. Maybe by the getaway vehicle.'

'Get forensics on to it,' Jane said.

An hour later, she was heading back to HQ. Her boss had been woken up and was on his way there from his home. He would want a report. She would ask him for more officers. He would start doing the sums. Everything cost money, and even murder came with a budget attached. Jane parked in an empty bay, just as a police van was drawing up. People were singing inside. Drunks, probably, on their way to a night in the cells. She pushed open the door to the police station and went in. The desk sergeant nodded and waved.

'Busy night?' he guessed.

'You heard about the shooting?'

He nodded. 'Thought it was funny, actually . . .'

She stared at him. 'Funny?'

'Odd, I mean. You know that Ray Masters has links to George Renshaw?'

'Bob told me.'

The desk sergeant smiled. 'Well, Bob knows everything, doesn't he?'

'Meaning I don't?'

'You're a quick learner, though, ma'am. So tell me this, who's Don Empson?'

She walked towards him. 'No idea,' she confessed.

'Only, we had him in here a few hours back. Patrol car picked him up in a graveyard. He spun them a story and we had to let him go.'

'So who is he then?' Jane asked.

'He's George Renshaw's right-hand man, that's who . . .'

Jane at the graveyard

As soon as it was daylight, Jane drove to the graveyard. The gates had been broken open. A chain and padlock lay on the ground next to them. The car was parked over towards a workman's hut. Empson had said it wasn't his. Fair enough. If he was telling the truth, his fingerprints wouldn't be all over the inside. She'd got the licence plate number from the officers who'd found Empson. The computer had come up with an owner's name and address, but the car had been sold by this man for spare parts.

Sold to George Renshaw. Now wasn't *that* a coincidence?

It wasn't much of a car. The paintwork was the only thing holding it together. She pushed a finger against an area of rust and the finger went straight through. She wiped the finger clean and took a walk around the graveyard. The grass was damp with dew. Birds were singing. She could count the number of clouds in the sky. She checked her watch. She had woken up someone from the council and asked them who would be in charge of the graveyard. He would meet her here. By now, he should have been here.

She kept walking. Behind a hedge she found a compost heap. There was a digger, too, and a wheelbarrow with a rake in it. The wheelbarrow had stains on it, not rust this time but something more like blood. Jane made a note to herself: get forensics down here. They could check the car at the same time. Maybe there'd be blood there too. As she continued her walk, she saw that back towards the gates the grass was stained. She crouched down. Again, it looked like blood. Someone had dripped blood along here. Someone wounded.

She retraced her steps, taking more care this time. She was looking for evidence. She was looking for something like a fresh grave. A sniffer dog might help . . .

Then she saw the man standing at the gates. He was examining them and shaking his head.

He saw her and started walking towards her, hands in pockets. There was a bag on his shoulder. Maybe it contained his work clothes and packed lunch. Jane introduced herself.

'Paul Mason,' he said, shaking her hand. 'A carjacking, was it? Boy racers?'

'A man in his late fifties, actually. At least, that's what we think. Can I take a look inside your shed?'

Mason nodded and led the way. He unlocked the shed and pulled open the door.

'Nothing's missing,' he said.

'What time did you leave work yesterday, Mr Mason?'

'Usual time. Five o'clock.'

'Do you work here alone?'

'I've got an assistant. I call him Gravy.'

'Gravy?'

'Short for graveyard. He was always hanging around this place. Never seen someone so pleased to be offered a job.'

'Was he here when you left?'

Mason nodded again. 'It's his job to tidy up and lock the gates.'

'So what time would he finish work?'

Mason laughed. 'He'd be here all hours if you let him. Gravy lives in a hostel. They sometimes have to come and fetch him. Time doesn't seem to mean anything to him . . .' Mason paused. 'He's not in trouble, is he?'

'I'll need to talk to him. Can you give me his address?'

'He'll be here in an hour or so. He's mad keen to get started in the morning.'

'I'll still need his address.'

It was in a folder in the hut, along with a telephone number. Jane punched the number into her phone. It took a while before anyone answered. She realised she didn't know Gravy's real name.

'Can I talk to Gravy, please?' she asked.

The sleepy-sounding man went away, but was back within thirty seconds. 'His bed's not been slept in,' he said, ending the call.

Jane stared at her phone. Mason asked if she was all right.

'Fine,' she assured him.

She wasn't so sure about Gravy, though.

'What's his real name?' she asked Mason.

'Jimmy Gray. Gray and Gravy, not so very different when you think about it.'

'He didn't go home last night.' She watched to see what kind of reaction she would get. Mason just made an O shape with his lips.

'Do you know a man called Donald Empson?'

she asked. Mason shook his head. 'How about George Renshaw?'

'Everyone knows him, at least by reputation.'

She nodded and wandered back in the direction of the car. It didn't belong to Empson, so why had he been driving it? And what kind of car did he usually drive? Jane reckoned it was time she had a word with Mr Donald Empson.

When she drove out to his home, however, the place was empty, the curtains looking as if they hadn't been shut the previous night. No sign of a car. It was a nice house, detached, modern. Husbands in suits were passing in the road, just starting to go to work. They must have wondered what she was up to, but none bothered to ask. Jane got back into her own car and decided on her next stop, Renshaw's scrapyard.

Jane at the scrapyard

A trailer was delivering two cars when she arrived. They had been involved in a crash of some kind, bonnets crumpled, radiator grilles smashed, windscreens shattered. She had been to plenty of accidents in her time. It was one of the worst things about the job. She gave a little shiver as she followed the convoy into the yard.

There were a couple of dogs barking nearby, but she couldn't see them. All she could see were dead cars. But then a man emerged from one of the buildings. He was chewing on a cigar. There was a scowl on his face as he neared the car. He had a shaved head, and gold rings on his fingers. Jane got out to meet him.

'I can smell bacon a mile off,' he growled.

'You must be Mr Renshaw?'

'Haven't seen you before.'

'I'm DI Harris.'

'Bit young.' He looked her up and down. Another man had emerged from the same building. He wore torn jeans and a red tartan shirt. He gave Jane a little whistle as he walked towards a nearby crane.

'I wonder if I can talk to Donald Empson,' she told Renshaw.

'He's not here.'

'Do you know where I could find him?'

'At home, maybe.'

'I've just come from there.'

Jane was staring at him. The nickname 'Gorgeous' was obviously a joke. He was one of the ugliest customers she'd ever met.

'What's this all about?' he asked. He had moved the cigar to a corner of his mouth, and bit down hard on it.

'A routine inquiry.'

Renshaw rolled his eyes. How many times had he heard the same line? The crane's motor was coughing into life.

'Will he be here later?' Jane shouted over the noise.

Renshaw just shrugged.

'Can I ask you what kind of car he drives?'

'Isn't that the sort of thing your computers can tell you?'

'Easier if I ask you.'

'That's what you think.' Renshaw gave a grin. Jane could feel that her phone was vibrating in her pocket. She took it out and held it to her ear, pushing a finger into her other ear to block out the noise. It was Bob.

'Got some news,' he said.

'Go ahead.'

'Door-to-door got lucky. They were talking to one of the neighbours and he asked them if they could do anything about the car that was blocking his skip. He's got a lorry coming this morning and it needs space so it can haul the skip away.'

'With you so far.' Jane had turned away from Renshaw so she could concentrate on the call.

'Well, the neighbour doesn't recognise the

car. It's bright green, some sort of sports model. It's legally parked, and most times we wouldn't bother, but this particular team is sharper than most. They ran a check. Car belongs to Mr Benjamin Flowers.'

'Don't tell me you know him?'

'I'm better than any computer, Jane, and I'm looking forward to that box of chocolates. Soft centres only, please.'

'I'm on my way to buy them, just as soon as you tell me who he is.'

'He's known as Benjy. He's Don Empson's nephew. And he works for Stewart Renshaw. Guess whose brother *he* is . . .'

Jane raised her eyes towards the sky. It was hard to take it all in. She saw that George Renshaw was looking up too. There was a huge magnet hanging from the arm of the crane. A large car swung from it. And though she could see mostly its underside and wheels, she thought she recognised the make. Ignoring Renshaw, and still holding her phone to her ear, she marched towards the crane.

'Shut it off!' she yelled.

The driver ignored her. She stuffed her phone back in her pocket and lifted out her warrant card, opening it and holding it up in front of the crane.

'I'm ordering you to shut it off!' she yelled. Then, turning towards Renshaw, 'Tell him!'

Renshaw hesitated, then waved a hand. The crane driver saw him and stopped the arm. Jane had just turned back to Renshaw when there was an explosion next to her. The car had landed not five feet from her. Dust and stones flew up. The car's windows blew out. Its tyres burst on impact with the ground. Her eyes blazed as she turned towards the crane operator.

'Thought that's what you wanted!' he yelled.

Her hand was shaking a little as she took out her phone again. She hadn't ended the call and Bob was asking what all the noise was. 'I need a forensics team at Renshaw's scrapyard,' she told him, as she circled what remained of the car. Quite a lot of it remained, actually. They made Bentleys to last. She was relieved that she'd ID'd it correctly. And now that she could see it, the licence plate matched the car taken from Raymond Masters', the murdered man's, garage. She wondered whose prints would be inside. She wondered what else might be in there. Nothing that she could see, but there was always the boot . . .

'So that's one forensics team still busy at the

garage,' Bob was saying, 'another wanted at the graveyard, and a third at the scrapyard. Tall order, Jane.'

'And while you're at it, how about checking the whereabouts of Mr Flowers?'

'Is that my quota for the day?'

Jane didn't answer. She was just realising that Renshaw had disappeared back into his office. She headed after him, walking into a single, chaotic room, at the far end of which was another door. The door was open. It led out into the scrapyard. When she went through it, a couple of guard dogs started snarling and straining against their leashes. They hadn't barked for their owner. They knew him too well.

George Renshaw was gone.

She cursed under her breath and started to search the scrapyard. He could be hiding anywhere, but she reckoned he wasn't that stupid. He was on foot, though, so she could follow in her car. But she couldn't leave the scene. The Bentley might vanish into thin air, just like Renshaw had done. Or prints could be wiped clean, evidence removed. She got Bob on the phone again.

'Donald Empson's car,' she told him. 'I need its details.'

'Hang on, I'll start a fresh list . . .' She could hear Bob sighing as he made a note to himself. 'Will that be all?'

'Not quite. George Renshaw has just done a runner on me.'

'I'll put the word out. Seems to me we might need some extra help.'

'I'll take it up with the boss.'

'You think Gorgeous George had Raymond killed?'

'I'm beginning to wonder.'

'With Don Empson pointing the gun? Or the nephew maybe?'

Jane didn't answer. She had reached in through a broken window and removed the Bentley's ignition key. Walking to the back of the car, she took a deep breath before unlocking the boot. It was empty. No visible traces of blood, and none that she could see on the steering wheel or either of the front seats. In fact, recent damage aside, it was pristine. Yet the shooter had lost blood, hadn't he? And Empson had sported no injuries when he'd been taken to the police station. Then there was the graveyard, the man called Gravy and his bed not slept in.

It didn't add up.

'Just tell forensics to get a move on,' she said into the phone.

Chapter Eight

Gravy's Story (3)

I liked the room. It was so clean, I almost didn't want to touch anything. After all, none of it really belonged to me. Celine was different. She was wearing the white robe from the bathroom and a pair of white slippers. She'd used the shower and opened the minibar. Not that we were sharing a room, mind! Separate rooms, but with a door between them. Adjoining rooms, the woman on the desk downstairs had said. This was 'one of the capital's most deluxe hotels'. It had a swimming pool and something called a spa. It had big televisions and a kettle and an iron and ironing board. It had magazines and a bowl of fruit on the table. I'd fallen asleep on my sofa, hadn't even managed to make it as far as the bed. When I woke up, Celine had been out shopping. She'd bought a clean shirt and trousers for me. The trousers were a bit too long, but fine at the waist. The shirt was fine, too. She told me I could stay for a day or two. 'Just until I make my plans.' But I wasn't to speak to anyone or phone anyone or go outside or anything.

'Just pretend you're on holiday.'

The view from my window was like something from a film, a big street and then Edinburgh Castle. There was a bar and a restaurant downstairs but Celine said I was to phone room service.

'Meals in your room, Gravy. Don't want anyone seeing you.'

I got the feeling that was why she kept the door between our rooms open. She was keeping an eye on me. She told me not to get any 'funny ideas'.

'Okay,' I said.

I'd already drunk all the tea and coffee in my room. She let me take some of hers. The red bag was in the wardrobe in her room. She said she would give me some money before we split up. Benjy's car was in the hotel garage. One of the hotel people had asked if I wanted it cleaned. I'd shaken my head.

'Sure?'

I was definitely sure. Sure, sure, sure, sure. Five times for luck.

Celine was lying along her sofa, drinking another of the tiny bottles from her minibar.

It was still morning. I wondered what my boss would be thinking. I wondered about the people I shared my house with. I had jobs that needed doing. I would lose a day's pay. My gloves were still in the car. What if someone broke in and stole them? I didn't even have the keys, one of the hotel people had kept them. That was bad, now that I thought about it. I stood in the doorway, staring at Celine. She was watching TV. People were in a room and they were shouting at each other. There was a man with a microphone who didn't seem to be helping.

'I need to fetch something from the car,' I told her.

'What?'

'My gloves. They're on the seat in the back.'

'What do you need them for?'

'I just do.'

'No you don't.'

'I do.'

She looked at me, then sighed. 'I'll come with you.'

'You don't need to.'

'Give me five minutes to get dressed.'

There were half a dozen big bags on the bed, all the clothes she'd bought. I nodded and went back into my room.

In fact, it took her more like fifteen minutes. She had put on some make-up and some perfume. She looked and smelled nice. 'Make sure you bring your key,' she said.

On our way down in the lift, she told me she wanted me to know something.

'Just in case anything happens to me.'

'What's going to happen?'

'Nothing, I hope. Train to London . . . but they'll be watching the stations, won't they? There's a boat from Rosyth to the continent, but I'd need a passport. I'm not sure yet, Gravy. There's got to be *some* place, hasn't there?'

'Lots of places,' I agreed.

'Somewhere I'll be safe. People want to hurt me, Gravy.'

'What people?'

'Well, maybe not hurt me, maybe just scare me.' The lift doors opened and we got out. She didn't say anything else. She asked the man behind the desk for the car key.

'We'll bring the car round, madam.'

'No, we just need to get something.'

So he went off and came back with the key. 'Bay twelve, madam.'

We started walking again. Out of the hotel and across a sort of courtyard. The car park was on the other side of this. It was concrete, several storeys high. Celine started talking again.

'I saw something I shouldn't have, Gravy. I was out walking by Brigham Woods. Do you know where that is? Edge of the city. I was trying to clear my head. A boyfriend had dumped me. Fair enough, it happens, but he'd taken up with someone I knew. Someone I thought was a pal. And how could I ask them?'

'Ask them what?'

'How long it had been going on.'

'A walk is good when you want to think,' I agreed.

'Bad timing, though. There was a car, see. Three men in it. I got a good look at them. Couple of days later, it's in the papers. "Body found in Brigham Woods." So I went to the cops. I was just . . . I dunno, I just thought how amazing to be part of that, to know something that could change everything. Do you know what I mean?'

'Maybe.'

We were walking up the slope into the car park. It was dim in there. There were numbers on the floor. Bay twelve, we wanted . . .

'I could ID the men, you see. And it turns out one of them was the victim, and the other two work for a man called George Renshaw. He's a villain, Gravy, and his second-in-command is called Don Empson. The police showed me their photographs. It was sort of too late by then, even though I knew I was in deep. I tried telling them I couldn't be sure, not a hundred per cent sure. I said I wasn't going to testify in court. But they kept on at me. Then they told me it might be best if I moved out of my flat for a while. I knew what that meant, it meant they were on to me . . .'

'Who?'

'Renshaw and Empson, plus the other two, the ones I'd ID'd. And the thing is, there's no way I'm going to go to court. Cops would have to drag me there screaming.'

'Well then,' I said, trying to comfort her. 'That's all right then. Just tell them that.'

'Right,' she said, giving me another of her looks. Then she pointed. 'Here's the car . . . Don Empson's car. I still can't work out how your pal Benjy got hold of it.'

'He was *your* pal too,' I reminded her. She gave a little twitch of the mouth.

'Go get your precious gloves,' she said, clicking the button to make the locks snap open. She'd turned her back, arms folded, head bowed. I think she was feeling sorry for herself. I could see my gloves. But when I reached into the car, I felt beneath the driver's seat until I found what I was really looking for, the blue plastic bag. The balaclava came out too, but I pushed it back into hiding. I placed my gloves in the bag and closed the door after me.

'Happy now?' she asked.

'Happy,' I agreed.

She had her mind on other things. All the way back to our rooms, not once did she ask where the blue bag had come from.

Chapter Nine

Bob Sanders Meets a Bent Cop

Bob Sanders didn't like visiting other cop shops. He always felt he was being judged by his fellow officers. He knew what they might be seeing, a guy close to retirement, a guy on his way to the scrapheap, a guy who should have done better. But Bob knew he was good at his job. The only reason he hadn't been promoted was that he had made enemies. If he didn't like you, he told you so to your face. If he didn't like your way of running things, he told you to your face. Not everybody was happy with that.

He'd been on the force for years, so was well known, if not always well liked. He pushed open the door of the cop shop and walked up to the desk, pressed the bell to let someone know he was there. When they arrived, he showed them his warrant card and asked to speak to Detective Sergeant Connolly. DS Connolly didn't invite him up to the CID office, he came downstairs to meet him instead.

Connolly was in his early thirties and looked tough but jaded, the sort of officer who should have found himself a different job. Being a cop had become too easy. Connolly shook Bob's hand and asked him what the problem was.

'You're assuming it's a problem,' Bob said with a thin smile.

'When isn't it?'

Connolly asked if they could move outside. The day was bright and windy. On the pavement, he lit a cigarette. Bob had turned down the offer of one. Bob stood there, waiting for Connolly to get comfortable. But that wasn't going to happen.

'I'm interested in a BMW,' Bob said. 'I asked the comms centre to send out the licence number, and guess what they told me? They said it had already been done. I found that a bit odd, so I asked them when, why and who. Last night, it turns out, and the one asking was you, DS Connolly.'

Connolly inhaled some smoke and held it there, releasing it down his nostrils. He gave a shrug by way of an answer.

'I'm assuming you know,' Bob went on, 'that the car in question is owned by a man called Donald Empson. It might tie him to a shooting at a garage yesterday. But the team only just got hold of that, while *you* seem to have a crystal ball tucked away somewhere.' Bob paused, but Connolly was still concentrating on the cigarette. 'Now, unless you want me going higher up with this, and by "higher up" I mean all the way to the top, I want to hear your side of the story. Might be, we can keep it between ourselves. Might be, you won't lose your job and your pension.'

It was the sort of threat Bob knew Connolly would react to. The man puffed out his cheeks before speaking.

'It was a favour.'

'Who for, Don Empson?' Bob watched as Connolly nodded. 'So someone's taken his car and he wants it back. Did he mention the shooting?'

'He said there might be someone wounded.'

'The guy in the garage is dead.'

'I think he meant whoever has his car.'

'And you kept this to yourself?' Bob got right into Connolly's face. 'You're worse than they are, do you know that?'

Connolly met the stare. 'I've known it for years,' he said, flicking away the remains of the cigarette and heading back into the cop shop.

Bob took out his phone and called Jane with the news.

Councillor Hanley's house

Lorna Hanley had woken up that morning at seven. Her husband Andrew wasn't in the bed. Putting on her dressing gown, she opened the door of his study a couple of inches and found him in his chair, asleep in his clothes. His mobile phone was beeping, telling him he had messages. His neck was at an awkward angle, and she knew he would be stiff when he woke up.

Downstairs, she made tea for herself and unloaded the dishwasher. There were only two Weetabix left, so she made a note to buy more, then dumped the empty packet in the bin. The bin was nearly full, so she hauled out the bag and tied it in a knot, replacing it with a fresh one. This was supposed to be Andrew's job, and like so many of Andrew's jobs she always ended up doing it herself. She had the radio playing as she ate breakfast. There was a report about another shooting. There were so many of them these days in the city. A garage owner was dead. The report stated that 'one or more assailants' might be on the run, and injured. She tutted and unlocked the kitchen door, taking the bin bag with her. When she opened the garden bin, she saw that there was a pair of shoes inside.

74

They were Andrew's shoes, his perfectly good shoes. Well, perfect apart from the paint, but paint could be removed.

She had shopping to do, and reckoned she could find a shoe repair shop. Maybe they'd be able to help. She placed the shoes in a carrier bag and decided to put them in the car so she wouldn't forget. She had started to forget things, which was why lists were such a good idea.

'You've too much on your plate, girl,' she told herself.

But when she went out front to the car, she saw that there was a dent to the back bumper. No wonder Andrew had been in a mood last night, someone had banged into his beloved Jaguar! She tutted again and unlocked the doors. Yesterday's newspaper was on the passenger seat. She swapped it for the shoes and took it into the house with her, ready for recycling. But Andrew had scrawled something in the margin of the front page. Maybe it was important. She placed her glasses on her nose and read the message.

RAYMOND'S GARAGE, 4 p.m., Empson/cash.

Lorna Hanley stared at the words as though they were written in some foreign language.

She heard a noise in the doorway. Andrew was standing there, rubbing at his face.

'You were there,' she told him, her voice trembling. 'You were at that garage, the one where the man was shot.'

He blinked at her. His mouth opened, and then closed itself again. Husband and wife locked eyes for a few moments. She was ready to hear his denial, but instead he turned and ran, leaving the front door wide open. She watched him go. She even stepped outside, to see where he might be heading, but he was gone. Back indoors, she finished her cup of tea, staring at nothing in particular. Then she lifted the telephone. Other wives might not do it, but she'd been brought up differently. She knew it was the right thing.

'Hello?' she said into the receiver. 'Police . . . ?'

Chapter Ten

Gorgeous George Phones his Brother

'Stewart? Is that you?'

'Who else would it be? What's the matter?'

Gorgeous George Renshaw was out of breath. He'd managed to flee the scrapyard and disappear into the maze of streets nearby. He knew he had to talk to his lawyer, but for some reason he'd called his brother instead. He was heading towards a café he knew. It was only two blocks further up the hill.

'Are you *walking*?' Stewart sounded amazed.

'A cop came to see me.'

'So?'

'So she recognised one of the cars. Don took it from Raymond's. I was just getting rid of it.'

'So it ties Don to the scene of the shooting?'

'And me with him!'

'All you have to say is that you don't know anything about it. Don Empson came to you with a car he wanted turned into scrap. You know him of old, so you felt you had to oblige.'

'That's good,' George said quietly. He knew now why he had called Stewart. Stewart was always the one with the ideas.

'So now I've done you a favour, maybe you can do one for me and get my money back from whoever took it!'

'Don's on the case.'

'Of course he is. Until the cops pull him in . . .'

George had reached the café. Its door opened with a little ping of a bell. The owner knew him, nodded and smiled. George took the table by the window, phone still pressed to his ear.

'Where is he anyway?' Stewart was asking. 'His nephew's still not turned up for work.' There was the sound of another phone ringing at Stewart's end. He told George to hang on while he took it. George stared out of the window, wondering how the world could look the same as always when his own personal universe was exploding. It was less than a minute before Stewart came on again. 'That was the cops,' he said. 'They want to know where they can find Benjy.'

'He's not turned up yet?'

'No.' Stewart fell silent, until George began to fear the connection had been lost. But then he heard his brother exhale loudly. 'Hold on a second,' Stewart said. 'How did the cops find you, George? How come they put two and two together so fast?'

'I don't know.'

'Don left the car with you, next thing you know, the cops are on to it. Meantime, nobody's seen Benjy since yesterday lunchtime. Do you see what I'm getting at? It's Don.'

'What is?'

'The cash! A little retirement present to himself. He's been wanting out of the firm ever since the old man died. So he sets the whole thing up. Goes to hand over the cash but has Benjy waiting in the wings . . .'

'Don wouldn't do that.' George's head was spinning. A mug of strong tea had appeared on the table and he ladled sugar into it. More ended up on the table than in the mug.

'Come on, George, think about it!' Stewart was saying.

George was trying to think. It wasn't easy. There was a hissing noise in his ears and his heart was pumping. Don hadn't tried stopping the shooter. Don hadn't gone after him. Don had left the Bentley for George to get rid of.

Don was out there somewhere with Sam and Eddie.

'You really think . . .'

Oh yes, Stewart really thought. 'Do you have any idea where he is now?'

'Going after Celine Watts. He's got Sam and Eddie with him.'

'And who are they working for, George? You or Don?'

'They're my guys.'

'Then tell them to bring Don in. We'll have a few words with him, see what he has to say.'

George nodded. 'Meantime, what about Hanley?'

'I've not tracked him down yet. Might have to pay a house call.'

'He'll be bricking it.'

'To start with, yes. But eventually, he's going to start asking for the money again.'

'You'll get your money back, Stewart.'

'I know I will, little brother. I know I will.'

Bob Sanders has news for Jane

Bob Sanders was on the phone to Jane again.

'Where are you?' he asked her.

'Just leaving the scrapyard.'

'So a team turned up, then?'

'At long last, yes. Any news on Empson and his BMW?'

'No, but listen to this. A woman decided to call 999.'

'That *is* strange.'

'Her husband is Andrew Hanley. He's on the council. In fact, he's Head of Planning.'

'I'm with you so far.'

'Mr Hanley came home last night with blood on his shoes. Guess where he'd been?'

'Where?'

'Raymond's Garage.' Bob paused. 'For a meeting with Donald Empson and an unknown amount of cash.'

Jane whistled. 'Is he hurt?'

'His wife doesn't think so. He told her the blood was paint.'

'So if he's not hurt, and Empson's not hurt, we're still one short.'

'And Benjamin Flowers still hasn't put in an appearance. Maybe Mr Hanley can fill us in.'

'Where is he now?'

'Well, according to his wife, he fled the house when she confronted him. I'm guessing it may tie in with some other calls we've been getting about a man, no jacket and no shoes, running hell for leather through Murison Park.'

'Is a patrol car on its way there?'

'Yes.'

'What would I do without you, Bob?'

'Save a fortune on confectionery,' he answered.

Don Empson is in trouble

Sam and Eddie were hungry. They were almost always hungry. That was why they'd pulled into a lay-by on the ring road. There was a snack van parked there. Don Empson could smell fried onions.

'Best burgers in the city,' Eddie had said. Despite which, Don had said he wasn't hungry. He swallowed another three pills instead, washing them down with water from a bottle. His stomach was on fire. 'Try to keep your stress levels down at work,' the doctors had advised. Some chance. He'd bought the water when they'd stopped for petrol. He had tried phoning his police contact again, but Connolly hadn't picked up. Dead ends, everywhere he looked.

He hoped Benjy was holed up somewhere and being looked after. It was Don's own fault. The boy had never been right for the job. There had always been little plans and notions, quick-money schemes. More than once, Don had covered his nephew's backside. There were gambling debts, poker games gone wrong. And expensive girlfriends to go with that flash car he drove. Weekends in five-star hotels. Wrong, all of it.

Don's own fault.

The best he could hope for was to get the money back pronto, then try to smuggle Benjy out of the country. That was the only option, or else he was dead meat. This was what Don was thinking as he stared out through the windscreen. Sam and Eddie were chomping their way through the burgers, kicking at stones, laughing about something. Not a care in the world, so it seemed. When Don's phone rang, he reached into his pocket for it.

He was wrong.

Not his phone, *hers*. He reached into his other pocket. He didn't recognise the number on the screen. He knew better than to answer, his voice might scare off whoever was on the other end. Instead, he let the phone ring. And when it stopped, he waited until the screen told him he had 1 Missed Call.

Followed a few moments later by 1 New Message.

Don punched the numbers and pressed the

phone to his ear. It was Celine Watts' voice. She was calling her own phone.

'Donna?' she began, meaning her cousin, obviously. 'Look, I hope you get this. Your own phone's out of credit. Sorry I ran off like that, but I just want you to know I'm all right. I've got to get away for a bit, that's all. Came into some cash, too, but relax, I'll see you get some.' Don's fingers tightened around the phone. He knew whose money it was. 'Anyway, just wanted you to know. I'll call you again, once I know where I'm going. Take care.' An electronic voice replaced Celine's, 'Message ends.' Don stared at the phone's screen and then punched some numbers in, the same numbers that had come up when Celine made the call.

A switchboard answered. 'Mansion Park Hotel, how may I direct your call?'

Don thought about that question for a second. Then he decided. 'I just need your address,' he said, slapping his hand against the horn, letting Sam and Eddie know playtime was over. But Sam was holding up one finger. He had a call of his own and needed to answer it. He spoke a couple of words, then did a lot of listening. Not that Don Empson noticed, he was too busy jotting down the details of the hotel.

When Sam got back into the driving seat, first thing he said was, 'We've got to head back to base.'

'No way,' Don argued. 'I've just got Celine Watts' address.'

'Really?'

'Yes, really. And it means we're going to Edinburgh.'

Sam seemed to hesitate. 'Boss wants us back home.'

Don was shaking his head. He took out his own phone and punched in Gorgeous George's number, started talking as soon as the call was answered.

'George, I know where Celine Watts is, and I think she's got the bag.'

There was silence for a moment. 'Is that a fact, Don?'

George didn't sound right somehow. Don found himself frowning. 'What's the matter?' he asked.

'You're coming back here, Don. Few questions that need answering.'

Don's heart sank. 'Look, George, I can fix this. Really I can.'

'So where's the money?'

'Mansion Park Hotel in Edinburgh. Celine Watts has it.'

'Have you been drinking, Don?'

'Her name and address were in my car. Guy called Gravy ended up with it and thought Watts had to be a friend of . . .' Don choked back the final word.

'Friend of Benjy's?' George said.

'Yes,' Don muttered. The truth was finally out.

'You saying this was his idea and not yours?' George was asking.

'It's nothing to do with me!'

'The boys will bring you back here, Don, and we can sort it all out.'

Don didn't know what to say to that. George was asking him to pass the phone to Sam. He did as he was told. He could hear what George was saying. They were to take Don to a pub George owned. Put him in the cellar. Keep an eye on him. George would be along later. 'Just as soon as I've checked out his story.'

Sam started the car. 'Something you want to tell us?' he asked Don, passing his phone back to him. Don pocketed it.

'Not your business, lads. But Celine Watts most definitely *is*. I thought you'd want her stopped. She's on the run, with a wedge of cash. If we don't set off after her right now . . .'

'That's not what the boss wants, Don.'

'He isn't always right, you know.'

Sam nodded slowly. 'All the same . . .'

All the same, Don knew which way the car would go. They were heading back towards Glasgow and a showdown.

Chapter Eleven

Jane and Bob Share Information

Patrol cars were on the hunt for George Renshaw. His usual lawyer had been told that the police wanted a word. But Jane knew that if Renshaw wanted to disappear, he would find it easy, in the short term at least.

She was back at the station. Andrew Hanley was in an interview room. He'd been reluctant to say anything, until told about the blood-stained shoes and the damage to his car. It would be a simple enough matter to match any flecks of paint to the car he'd reversed into on the garage forecourt. Then there was the newspaper with the meeting jotted down on it.

'I want to talk to my solicitor,' Hanley had stated, head in hands, a cold cup of coffee on the table in front of him.

'Your wife's in the next room, Mr Hanley. Do you want a word with her too?'

Bob and Jane met in the corridor. They had big smiles for one another.

'I'm going to be Willy Wonka by the end of this,' Bob said. Jane patted his arm.

'We're not out of the woods yet.'

'No, but we're getting there.' He held up a slip of paper. The list of tasks she had given him. 'Initial forensic report, same fingerprints on the Bentley and the car in the graveyard. Probably Don Empson's, but that'll take a bit longer to confirm. Blood and brain matter on one wing of the Bentley, Raymond's, I'm pretty sure. And by the way, the Bentley's owner's not too happy with the valet job.'

Jane smiled and folded her arms, knowing there was more to come. Bob checked his list again.

'Blood in the graveyard is the same group as one of the pools in the garage. Again, we're waiting for a DNA match.'

'But no blood in the graveyard car?'

'No.'

'And none inside either the Bentley or Benjamin Flowers' abandoned sportster?'

Bob shook his head. 'But Benjy's employer says he's gone AWOL.'

'Our wounded gunman? Missing, along with some cash and Empson's BMW.'

'Find one and we probably find all three.'

'What about this guy who works at the grave-yard, how does he fit in?'

Bob shrugged. 'Maybe he doesn't. But a pound to a penny says it comes down to Stewart Renshaw.'

Jane's eyes narrowed. 'How so?'

'Word is, he's got a new casino looking for planning permission.'

'Has he now?' Jane thought for a moment. 'But he's on the straight and narrow, isn't he?'

'We've never had proof to the contrary, if that's what you mean.' Bob pursed his lips.

'Well, well.' Jane folded her arms, deep in thought. 'Hanley goes to the garage to pick up a bribe. It goes wrong somehow.'

'Somebody got greedy.'

'Benjamin Flowers?' She nodded slowly. 'I'd still like to get my hands on Don Empson,' she said.

'You need to be patient.'

She stared at him. 'Meaning what?'

'Meaning putting the team to work. Stake out anywhere George Renshaw or Don Empson might turn up. At least one of them's got to be on the hunt for Benjy, and my guess would be Empson.'

'Hunting his own nephew?'

It was Bob's turn to nod.

'So all we can do is wait?' she asked.

'All we can do is wait,' Bob confirmed.

Gorgeous George needs a taxi

It was a short walk from the café to the taxi office. George didn't go there much, even though he owned the place. Owned all the taxis, too. He had someone else fronting the operation for him, but it was his money behind it, and him raking in the profits. Taxis, his dad had told him, were useful. You could use them for ferrying merchandise and people around the city and further afield. Nobody looked twice at a taxi. George was there because he needed a bit of ferrying himself. His car was at the scrapyard. There was no way he could go back for it. He had two more cars in the garage at his house, but he reckoned police would be waiting for him there too. So instead, he would use a taxi. As he walked into the office, the three drivers stood up. So did the woman who was working the telephone. Magazines and newspapers hit the floor. Mugs of tea trembled in their hands.

One thing they all knew. Somebody was in trouble.

'Easy,' George reassured them, holding his palms up. 'Nothing to worry about, I just need a lift somewhere.'

All three were willing, pretended to be eager even. George pointed to the nearest one. 'You'll do,' he said.

Out at the taxi, the driver unlocked the doors and asked where they were going.

'Edinburgh,' he was told.

He nodded, trying to hide his surprise. That was the rest of his shift taken care of. Having climbed into the back, George was already busy with his phone. He wanted to talk to Sam and Eddie, wanted to make sure they were getting things right for once. He saw the driver fiddling with something and leaned forward in his seat.

'Am I seeing things,' he growled, 'or did you just put the meter on?'

'Force of habit,' the driver said, switching it off again.

So busy were driver and passenger that, as the taxi roared out of the parking lot, neither noticed the unmarked police car as it reversed into a tight parking space. The two detectives in the car looked at one another.

'Was that him?' one asked.

His partner replied with a nod. Their car did a U-turn and got ready to follow the black cab at a distance.

Chapter Twelve
Gravy's Story (4)

I was going to miss Celine.

'I've only just learned to say your name the right way,' I told her.

She was emptying the red bag into a suitcase. It was one of those posh ones with wheels and a handle. When she came back from the shops with it, she brought me a present: one of Celine Dion's CDs.

'That who you're named after?' I asked.

'Suppose so,' she said, busy with the suitcase again. She was going to go on a train. It was a special train that left Edinburgh last thing at night and arrived in London next morning. She'd explained that you got a bed and you could sleep all the way there.

'Sounds nice, Celine. Why can't I come?'

But she shook her head. 'Safer for you if you stay here.'

'You said they'd be watching the stations.'

'That's a chance I've got to take.'

'There's always the car.'

'It's Don Empson's car, Gravy. Do you think they won't be looking for it?'

Then she folded some of the money and stuck it in my trouser pocket. 'You've been a good friend, Gravy,' she said, and that made me blush. She'd paid for another night at the hotel, both rooms. It meant she wouldn't be noticed as missing. She wanted me to stay the night, and in the morning I could do anything I wanted.

'Breakfast's included,' she told me.

'And after that I can go home?' I watched her nod. 'You think I should leave the car here?'

'Up to you.' She looked up at me. 'Time you started taking some decisions, Gravy.'

'I will,' I said. The TV in her room had a clock on it. 'Your train's not for hours.'

'I know.'

'But you're leaving just now?'

She nodded. 'I'm fed up hanging around.'

'We could go to a film,' I blurted out. She gave me a look and a smile.

'I've got a taxi coming.'

'I could run you to the station.'

But she shook her head again. 'Better this way,' she said.

'Why? Why is it better?'

'It just is.' She was beginning to sound irritated. I know that happens with people. It happens with the people in my house. I ask one question too many and they sound like that. How does the moon shine? What happens when we die?

'Celine,' I said, but she was zipping the case shut.

'Got to go,' she told me. She slipped into her jacket. It was brand new. Everything about her looked new. She tucked her hair into a beret. 'I'm trying for the foreign tourist look,' she explained.

'I've never been to London.'

'I'll send you my address.'

'Promise?'

'Promise.' And then she kissed me on the cheek, and I went redder than ever. I could see myself in the mirror. My face was on fire. Not exactly a cool head, Gravy. The door clicked after her. The room was silent, but I could still smell her perfume. It took me a minute to realise that she didn't have my address! I opened the door, but she wasn't in the corridor. Well, I'd told her about the graveyard, a letter would always find me there. I lay on her bed for a while, staring at myself in the TV screen. She had taken all the stuff from the minibar and her bathroom. Supplies for the journey, she'd said. There was a price list for the minibar. It was on the bedside table. Would I have to pay for it in the morning? Maybe that was why she'd given me the money.

I took the notes out of my pocket and tried counting them. Fifteen, or nearly fifteen. Times twenty. That was a lot. The red bag was on the carpet, empty now. In my own room I had the blue carrier bag. It was on the top shelf in the wardrobe. I could put the Celine Dion CD in there. So that was what I did. Then I made myself a cup of tea, using the last of the tea bags and milk. I lay on my own bed, one foot crossed over the other, three big pillows behind my head. There wasn't much on the TV. On one of the channels, they all spoke a language I didn't know. But I recognised the show. I was sure I'd seen it in English.

The minutes crept by. Maybe she would come back. Maybe she would miss me, or miss her train. Maybe she'd forgotten something. I looked again in her room, but didn't find any-thing. I knew where her cousin lived, and that was a start. She would phone her cousin. Blood was blood, my mum used to say. She would phone her cousin and I'd be there visiting and the cousin would hand the phone over to me. And that would be us, friends again.

The phone in her room rang and I ran through to pick it up. Who else could it be but her?

'Hello?'

But then the phone went dead. I listened for a while longer, but it stayed dead. Well, at least she'd tried calling. I stared out of the window at the evening. The castle was lit up. There were people on the street. They looked like they were having fun. Life was all about fun, wasn't it? That was when I realised I was bored.

'Never mind the breakfast,' I said to myself. On the other hand, what if she *did* come back and I wasn't there? See, I was thinking about heading home. But I'd promised I would stay, just one last night. Yes, but I was bored and I needed some fresh air. I could go for a drive and still come back. Or a walk. I could walk, same as the people outside were doing. Celine had teased me that there were bars on the street where naked girls danced, but I wouldn't go there. I looked around her room and then mine, and decided to take my blue carrier bag. What else did I have?

Oh, my room key. I couldn't forget that.

When I went into the corridor, there was a

man standing there. He was standing outside Celine's door. He looked at me.

'Hello,' I said. He just nodded. 'Do you work here?'

'That's right, sir,' he said with a smile.

'She's not in.'

He stared at me. 'And how do you know that, sir?'

'Connecting rooms,' I explained.

'And your name is?'

'Everyone calls me Gravy. That's because I work at the graveyard.'

'And you're here with . . . ?'

'Celine. She's named after Celine Dion.'

The man nodded. He was coming towards me. He stopped just short. 'Well, Don was telling the truth for once. Do you know when she's coming back? I've got a message for her.'

'I can take it, if you like,' I offered.

'It's really for her, sir.'

I looked him up and down. He didn't look like he worked for the hotel. Everyone wore a kind of uniform and a name badge. And he'd used the name Don. I'd heard that name just recently.

He had leaned forward, so his face was right next to mine. 'Where's my money?' he hissed.

I stared at him. 'I don't know.'

'I think you do, Gravy. The red bag.'

'It's empty.'

'So she's got the cash?'

'The money belongs to Benjy, and Benjy wanted her to have it. She's nice.'

He glared at me. 'I'm going to ask you one last time . . . Where's Benjy? Where's the car? And where's that tart gone with my money?'

I managed not to blink. Everything was blurry at the edges, but then it wasn't. It was really sharp instead. 'The car park,' I said.

'Take me.' He gave me a little shove in the direction of the lifts. Well, what else could I do? He wanted me to, so I took him.

Chapter Thirteen
Jane is in Edinburgh

'The Mansion Park Hotel,' Jane said into her phone. She was parked outside. The taxi was about twenty yards away, the driver chatting away on his own phone, paying no mind to anything else.

'In Edinburgh?' Bob's voice asked.

'That's the one.'

'His idea of hiding out?'

'Who knows.' Jane shifted in the driver's seat. As soon as she'd got word that George Renshaw was on the move, she'd set off after him. And as soon as she had caught up with the car tailing him, she'd radioed to tell the other car it could pull back. A two-car tail was perfect, meant you could keep swapping, meaning less chance of the car you were following spotting you. The two CID men were parked around the other side of the hotel, just in case.

'Is Andrew Hanley talking?'

'He is,' Bob confirmed. 'Remember what I said about Stewart Renshaw's casino?'

'You were right?' she guessed.

'Only one hundred per cent.'

'Yet I'm the one who got the promotion.' Jane was smiling.

'Bit more good news, if you're up for it.'

'Days like this don't happen nearly often enough, Bob.'

'Two of Gorgeous George's boys, the two we've been after for the Brigham Woods murder, turned up about forty minutes ago.'

'Yes?'

'They marched Donald Empson into one of George's pubs. When our stake-out team sauntered in, pretending to be customers, there was no sign of any of them. The cellar looks a good bet.'

'Empson screwed up, and he's about to pay the price?'

'I don't want to go charging in until we're sure.'

Jane nodded to herself. 'I agree. Maybe it's something I can talk to Renshaw about.' She saw movement at the hotel doors. Two men making their exit. 'Hold on,' she said into the phone. 'Something's happening. I'll have to call you back.'

'Jane?' Bob was telling her as she ended the call. 'Remember, look after number one . . .'

Gravy and Gorgeous George

The two men crossed the tarmac, heading for the multi-storey car park. Gravy was taller than George Renshaw by a couple of inches. Thinner, too. He carried the blue carrier bag. Renshaw signalled to the driver of his taxi. Everything's going to plan. Keep the engine running. This won't take long. On the way down in the lift, he had pulled on a pair of tight leather gloves, an idea borrowed from Don Empson. He flexed his hands as he walked.

'So you're a mate of Benjy's?' Renshaw was asking. 'How's he doing?'

Gravy just shrugged.

'How did he ever think he'd get away with it?'

Another shrug.

'And Don. You do know Don, don't you?'

A shake of the head.

'You don't know Don?'

'I know it's his car.'

'So how exactly do *you* fit in, Mr Gravy?'

'It's just "Gravy", not "Mr Gravy".'

103

'Whatever. Which floor are we going to?'
They were entering the car park.

'This one,' Gravy said.

The level was only half full, and Renshaw spotted Don Empson's BMW straight away. He gave a low whistle, almost jogging towards it.

'I tried cleaning up the blood,' Gravy was explaining. 'I did my best.'

'Sure you did, kid,' Renshaw said. He rubbed a gloved hand over the car and peered inside. Then he turned to Gravy. 'So?'

'The boot,' Gravy said.

'Got the key?'

Gravy nodded.

'Give it here then.'

The key changed hands. Renshaw pressed the button and the boot clicked open half an inch. He yanked it all the way up and stood there, mouth hanging open. Benjy's body was curled into a ball. It was swelling and leaking and starting to smell. Renshaw began to cough. He took a step back, then turned towards Gravy. Gravy was holding the blue bag. He was pointing it at Renshaw. Then he pulled the trigger and the bag exploded. The kick sent the gun flying from Gravy's hand. Renshaw winced and went down on one knee, then fell backwards, clutching his right leg. The bullet had gone into his upper thigh. Blood was pumping out. Renshaw's face was screwed up in pain. Gravy knelt down and touched the man's forehead.

'Warm,' he said. 'Warm, warm, warm, warm.' Five times for luck. Then, curious, he touched the man's chest. Stood to reason. If the head was warm, then the heart should be cold.

Stone cold.

But it wasn't.

People were coming. A woman and two men, running. Gravy didn't know them. He stood up, and one of the men shouted for him to step away from the vehicle. Gravy was happy to do that. The woman was walking slowly towards him. The other man was phoning for an ambulance. The woman glanced inside the boot of the car, then she locked eyes with Gravy.

'My name's Detective Inspector Harris,' she said.

'Mine's Gravy.'

'Yes, I know. What are you doing here, Gravy? You're a long way from home.'

Gravy nodded his agreement with this.

'Are you working for Don Empson?' she asked.

Gravy shook his head. 'I'm just Benjy's pal, that's all.'

'I'm guessing this is Benjy?' She meant the body in the boot. Instead of answering, Gravy looked over towards George Renshaw. Renshaw was clutching his wounded leg, cursing and swearing and making pained noises as he rolled around on the floor.

'I don't like swearing,' Gravy stated. 'My mum told me it's not clever.'

'Your mum was quite right.' DI Harris was studying the car. 'This belongs to Don Empson, doesn't it?'

Gravy nodded again. 'But I thought it was Benjy's. Can I go back to work now?' he asked.

Harris didn't answer straight away. She had her own phone out and was telling someone on the other end of it that they should enter the bar and check the cellar. Flicking the phone shut, she asked Gravy if he was sure he was all right.

'I'm fine,' he said. 'I didn't want to shoot him. I just didn't know what else to do. Benjy wanted me to hide the gun.' He looked at her. 'I'll get into trouble, won't I? I didn't do what he wanted.' He took a deep breath and gave a long, loud sigh.

'Is there any money, Gravy? I'm thinking there should be money.'

But Gravy was shaking his head. 'If you're

looking for Celine,' he told the detective, 'she's not here. I don't know where she went, so there's no use asking, is there?'

'Celine?' For the first time, the detective looked confused.

Gravy pointed to the ground where the remains of the blue bag had landed. There was a CD lying there. 'My fingers feel funny,' he said, studying them. 'I don't think I want to do any more shooting.'

'I'm glad to hear it.' Harris had crouched down to pick up the CD.

Gravy was pressing the palm of one hand against his chest. 'Warm heart,' he told the detective. 'That's got to be a good thing, hasn't it?'

Jane Harris nodded, but she was still left wondering . . . what on earth did Celine Dion have to do with any of this?

Quick Reads

Books in the Quick Reads series

101 Ways to get your Child to Read	Patience Thomson
All These Lonely People	Gervase Phinn
Black-Eyed Devils	Catrin Collier
The Cave	Kate Mosse
Chickenfeed	Minette Walters
Cleanskin	Val McDermid
A Cool Head	Ian Rankin
Danny Wallace and the Centre of the Universe	Danny Wallace
The Dare	John Boyne
Doctor Who: I Am a Dalek	Gareth Roberts
Doctor Who: Made of Steel	Terrance Dicks
Doctor Who: Revenge of the Judoon	Terrance Dicks
Doctor Who: The Sontaran Games	Jacqueline Rayner
Dragons' Den: Your Road to Success	
A Dream Come True	Maureen Lee
Girl on the Platform	Josephine Cox
The Grey Man	Andy McNab
The Hardest Test	Scott Quinnell
Hell Island	Matthew Reilly
How to Change Your Life in 7 Steps	John Bird
Humble Pie	Gordon Ramsay
Life's New Hurdles	Colin Jackson
Lily	Adèle Geras
One Good Turn	Chris Ryan
RaW Voices: True Stories of Hardship	Vanessa Feltz
Reaching for the Stars	Lola Jaye
Reading My Arse!	Ricky Tomlinson
Star Sullivan	Maeve Binchy
The Sun Book of Short Stories	
Survive the Worst and Aim for the Best	Kerry Katona
The 10 Keys to Success	John Bird
The Tannery	Sherrie Hewson
Twenty Tales from the War Zone	John Simpson

Quick Reads

Pick up a book today

Quick Reads are bite-sized books by bestselling writers and well-known personalities for people who want a short, fast-paced read. They are designed to be read and enjoyed by avid readers and by people who never had or who have lost the reading habit.

Quick Reads are published alongside and in partnership with BBC RaW.

We would like to thank all our partners in the Quick Reads project for their help and support:

Arts Council England
The Department for Innovation, Universities and Skills
NIACE
unionlearn
National Book Tokens
The Vital Link
The Reading Agency
National Literacy Trust
Welsh Books Council
Basic Skills Cymru, Welsh Assembly Government
Wales Accent Press
The Big Plus Scotland
DELNI
NALA

Quick Reads would also like to thank the Department for Innovation, Universities and Skills; Arts Council England and World Book Day for their sponsorship and NIACE for their outreach work.

Quick Reads is a World Book Day initiative.
www.quickreads.org.uk   www.worldbookday.com

Quick Reads

Reaching for the Stars
How you can make your dreams come true

Lola Jaye

Harper

'When I was eleven years old I used to shut myself away in my room and write, creating characters and imagining them on children's telly!'

Lola Jaye always dreamed of being a writer, but getting her first book published wasn't easy. She would come home from her day job and write every evening and weekend. But it wasn't until years later, after lots of rejections, that she finally got her first book deal.

Now Lola wants to help others reach for their dreams. In this step-by-step guide, she shows that, with plenty of self-belief and hard work anything is possible.

Quick Reads

The Dare
John Boyne

Black Swan

At the start of his school holidays, Danny Delaney is looking forward to a trouble-free summer. But he knows that something terrible has happened when his mother returns home one afternoon with two policemen.

There has been an accident. Mrs Delaney has hit a small boy with her car. The boy is in a coma at the local hospital and nobody knows if he will ever wake up.

Danny's mother closes herself off, full of guilt. Danny and his father are left to pick up the pieces of their broken family.

John Boyne tells the story from the point of view of a twelve-year-old boy. *The Dare* is about how one moment can change a family forever.

Quick Reads

Dr Who: The Sontaran Games
Jacqueline Rayner

BBC Books

Every time the lights go out, someone dies...

The TARDIS lands at an academy for top athletes, all hoping to be chosen for the forthcoming Globe Games. But is one of them driven enough to resort to murder? The Doctor discovers that the students have been hushing up unexplained deaths. As he begins to investigate, the Doctor finds a squad of Sontarans invading the academy!

As the Sontarans begin their own lethal version of the games, the Doctor is captured and forced to take part in the Sontaran Games. Can even a Time Lord survive this deadly contest?

Featuring the Doctor as played by David Tennant in the acclaimed hit series from BBC Television.

Quick Reads

All These Lonely People
Gervase Phinn

Penguin Paperbacks

The world is full of lonely people. One wonders where they all come from...

Even with a huge problem to worry about, Father McKenzie still manages to see the good in everyone. His job is made more difficult by his nosy housekeeper and the gossips from the shop down the road. Will they succeed in spoiling things, or will Father McKenzie's advice win the day?

This charming tale shows the ups and downs of everyday life in a truly heart-warming way. It will have you laughing out loud and shedding a tear – all at the same time.

Quick Reads

The Tannery
Sherrie Hewson

Pan

This is the story of one family struggling to survive the war years.

It's 1938. Dolly Ramsden is six years old. Times are hard. But Dolly doesn't care. Her family is everything to her.

Then war comes and everything changes. Her father leaves his job at the local tannery and joins the war effort. He leaves behind a bitter wife and a daughter who can see no hope for the future. With no money, Dolly's mother is forced to take desperate measures to help them survive. Soon she becomes lonely and depressed. She turns to drink and Dolly's life becomes a living hell.

When the war ends and Dolly's father comes home, he finds a teenage daughter who has grown up too soon, and a wife who has been destroyed by what she's become. Hatred and secrets hinder his attempts to restore a normal life for them. Until, one night, things get out of control....

Quick Reads

Black-Eyed Devils
Catrin Collier

Accent Press

One look was enough. Amy Watkins and 'Big' Tom Kelly were in love. But that one look condemned them both.

Amy's father is out to kill Tom. All Tom wants is Amy, but Tonypandy in 1911 is a dangerous place for Irish workers who have been brought in to replace the striking miners.

The miners drag them from their beds and hang them from lamp posts as a warning to those who would take their jobs. Frightened for Amy, Tom fights to deny his heart, while Amy dreams of a future with the man she loves. But her dream seems impossible until a man they believed to be their enemy offers to help. But, can they trust him with their lives?

Quick Reads

101 Ways to get your Child to Read
Patience Thomson
Foreword by Michael Morpurgo

Barrington Stoke

Some children find it hard to read. Some parents find it hard to help them. So how can you get your child reading if they can't read, or won't read? And what if you're not a great reader yourself? *101 Ways to get your Child to Read* has the answers.

This is an accessible and friendly book. It draws on Patience's thirty years of experience teaching reading, and her ten years of publishing books for reluctant readers. It features advice and encouragement from celebrity parents and well-known dyslexics. It also gives practical, tried-and-tested tips to help every parent to encourage their child to read.

Quick Reads

Dragons' Den
Your road to success

Duncan Bannatyne, Deborah Meaden,
Peter Jones, Theo Paphitis and James Caan

Collins

4 million people watch the Dragons on TV. Now you can read their stories and learn from them.

Duncan Bannatyne, Deborah Meaden, James Caan, Peter Jones and Theo Paphitis are the stars of TV programme *Dragons' Den*, but they haven't always been millionaires and TV stars. Here, they reveal the secrets that have taken them from nothing to the very top.

The Dragons tell their personal stories of success and failure. They also give advice on how to succeed in business and in life, including how to make money from scratch.

If you're looking for advice on making the most of your life or your business, this is the perfect book for you.

Other resources

Free courses are available for anyone who wants to develop their skills. You can attend the courses in your local area. If you'd like to find out more, phone 0800 66 0800.

 Don't get by get on 0800 66 0800

A list of books for new readers can be found on www. firstchoicebooks.org.uk or at your local library.

 The Vital Link

Publishers Barrington Stoke (www.barringtonstoke.co.uk), New Island (www.newisland.ie) and Sandstone Press (www.sandstonepress.com) also provide books for new readers.

 Barrington Stoke   OPEN DOOR    SANDSTONEPRESS CONTEMPORARY QUALITY READING

The BBC runs a reading and writing campaign. See www.bbc.co.uk/raw.

 RaW BBC